For Annalie – S. G.

To my sister, Kipa, with whom
I learnt to skate – H. H.

A CHRYSALIS CHILDREN'S BOOK

First published in Great Britain in 2003 by
Chrysalis Children's Books, an imprint of Chrysalis Books Group Plc
The Chrysalis Building
Bramley Road
London W10 6SP
www.chrysalisbooks.co.uk
This paperback edition first published in 2004

Text © Sally Grindley 2003
Illustrations © Heli Hieta 2003
Design and layout © Pavilion Children's Books 2003

The moral right of the author and illustrator
has been asserted

Designed by Sarah Goodwin

A CIP catalogue record for this book is available
from the British Library.

ISBN 1 84458 160 8

Set in Cochin

Printed in China

2 4 6 8 10 9 7 5 3 1

This book can be ordered direct from the publisher. Please contact
the Marketing Department. But try your bookshop first.

This book may be returned to any Wiltshire
library. To renew this book phone your library
or visit the website: www.wiltshire.gov.uk

Wiltshire
COUNTY COUNCIL

LM6.108.5

SKILLS FOR ALL

Polar Skater

Sally Grindley

Illustrated by Heli Hieta

Chrysalis Children's Books

I had longed for my skates,
Couldn't wait for my birthday,
Now I held them, crisp white leather,
Cutting edges crystal smooth.

"Put them on then," urged Dad,
But my fingers fumbled laces,
I froze by the rink side
Not daring to move.

Then I slithered and slid
Like a great ugly duckling,
Fear scrambled my senses
And tangled my steps.

I floundered and fell,
Stood up and fell down again,
I tried hard to laugh
But tears pricked at my eyes.

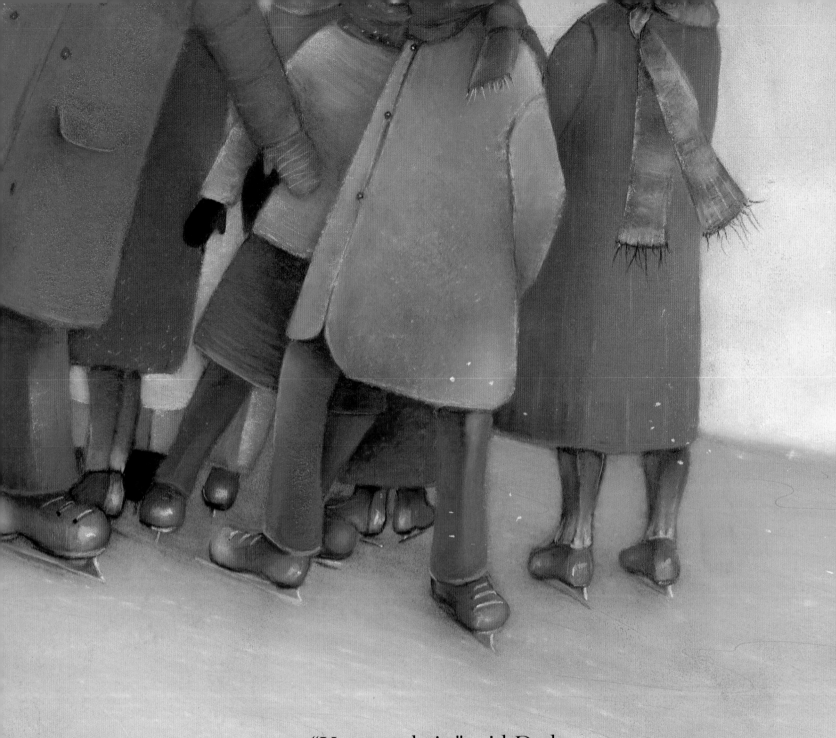

"You can do it," said Dad.
"Hold my hand and I'll help you."
I grabbed his hand fast
And gave him the lead.

We spun round the ice
In a whirlpool of colours,
Weaving through people
At breathtaking speed.

Then my hand lost his grip,
And the crowds overwhelmed me,
Sparks splintered the air
As I crashed my way out.

The sunlight was dazzling,
I blinked away blindness,
Till the world opened up
In a brilliance of white.

Mountains rose high,
Soft clouds brushed their snow caps,
I took my first steps
On an ocean of ice.

They were steps full of wonder.
"I can skate!" I cried out.
"I can skate, come and see!"

Seals bobbed round ice floes
And gazed at me wide-eyed,
Clapping their flippers
And barking with joy.

Walruses yawned
And back-scratched each other,
A heap of pink bellies
Warmed by the sun.

Polar bears ran with me,
Cubs slipped and tumbled,
Kicking up snow
With their powder-puff paws.

Above, long-tailed skuas
Swept arcs through wind currents,
I followed their trail,
Sewing patchworks in ice.

Then the whales came to watch me,
Bold belugas and bowheads
Chirped and squealed their curiosity,
Slapped their tails in the waking sea.

I leapt with the narwhals
Turned cartwheels and somersaults,
Saw them cleave through the water
When they dived down for food.

I rode with the caribou,
Bare-back over ice lakes,
Saw musk oxen nuzzling
Their newly-born calves.

White wolves were hunting,
Their haunting calls echoed,
A snowstorm disguised us
And kept them at bay.

One last leap of freedom
Propelled me through sundown
Past Arctic hares lazing
And snow geese at rest.

But now darkness hovered
And cold winds bit harder,
I had to go back
Before night slammed its doors.

I surrendered myself
Through the last glow of twilight
As the whales' drifting shadows
Plunged into the sea.

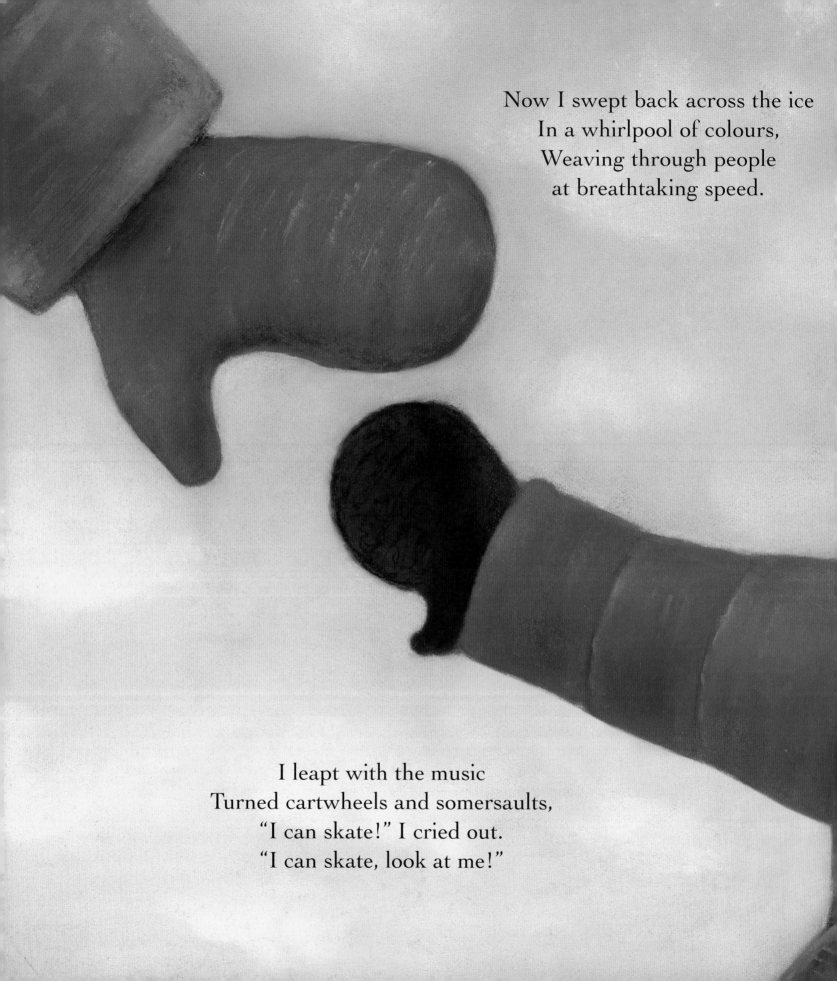

Now I swept back across the ice
In a whirlpool of colours,
Weaving through people
at breathtaking speed.

I leapt with the music
Turned cartwheels and somersaults,
"I can skate!" I cried out.
"I can skate, look at me!"